HEARTBEATS OF DELHI'S STREETS

Rahini Bansal

ISBN 979-8-89744-144-0

Dedicated to all those who feel lost on their own;
There will be paths to guide you home.

Epigraph

"Cities have the capability of providing something for everybody, only because, and only when, they are created by everybody."

— Jane Jacobs

CHAPTER 1

Khan Market. The heart of Delhi. The one place everyone feels at home. A vivid description of Khan Market resides in every Delhites' heart. Every description is not the same, but the essence doesn't change. Khan Market has everything from low cost shops to posh brands, from authentic italian food to the local north indian delicacies, from the well dressed working class to people trying to earn a day's food. The dogs lying on the cool footwalk, lazing the day away underneath the humid sunlight, the narrow roads leading to others, the vibrancy of variety and the faint voice of people, almost as background music.

It was just another morning, perhaps one to be more ecstatic about. I was going to Khan Market with my friends, contemplating which dress I should wear. Just as I combed the last of my hair, I heard the honking of a car resting in front of my house at the center of the crossing. They were already here to pick me up! That certainly caught me off guard considering they're always late. I ran down stairs, gulped a huge glass of water and rushed out to the car. On reaching Khan Market, our eyes wandered around trying to soak in the sights and sounds but to our surprise, nothing caught our eye, everything was the same old. A fight between two stores men and a bargaining woman, a few kids, merely 8 or 9 years old, selling notebooks and pens to earn merely 30 rs to pass the day, trash lying on the footwalk, a group of friends eating food at one of the eateries, a closed off construction sight, coffee spilt on the pebbly road etc. My eyes suddenly fell on the little kids, younger than us, who had nowhere to live and weren't even guaranteed proper meals for the day. It isn't as if this was my first time seeing them but something just made me stand there, not aware of my surroundings, and stare at them.

Khan Market

"Hey! What happened?" One of my friends called out.

I snapped out of my sudden trance unbothered and relished the day with my friends like no other. As soon as I got home, a certain uneasy feeling settled in the bottom of my heart. Thinking about our well spent day, I couldn't help but mull over those children and their innocent faces. What must they have to go through everyday? Why do we have such privileged lives whilst they have nothing? Why aren't they receiving the education they deserve?

This curiosity got the best of me and I got off my bed, called my friends, and got this feeling off my chest. My friends, genuinely concerned like me, helped think of a solution. We all put our heads together to think of what was the least we could do for these children that would affect their lives for the better and stir hopes for a better future. And then it struck us! Probably one of our more brilliant ideas. The next day we told our parents what we were aiming to do and our plan was in action! We rushed back to khan market and started looking for the children.

We found them and bought everything that they had to offer, notebooks, pens, pencils. This led to them making quite satisfactory earnings. They were delighted by their sales but didn't expect what was coming next.

When we had collected all their notebooks and pens, we distributed these notebooks amongst the children themselves. They looked up at us, with their innocent doe eyes, puzzled as to what we were doing. We could understand that they couldn't make out what our purpose was. We told them that they could keep the notebooks and pens because they were soon going to start studying.

"We have no mode of studying. Our parents can't afford to send us to school. That is why we've to make our earnings this way." One of the kids pointed out.

"That is why we will be teaching you." My friend got down on both knees to look at the child eye to eye and replied with a gracious, gentle smile on her face.

A certain smile spread across their faces which warmed our hearts entirely. We told them that one of us was going to come each week to teach them important parts of different subjects. They jumped around with pure happiness, one not only on their faces but in their hearts. Happiness that spreads at the opportunity of education.

We gave them their first lesson, mathematics, together in a calm place without any chaos or disturbance. A few children started crying at the thought of this opportunity that they would've completely missed out on due to the environment they were born in. We still needed polishing upon how we teach but we picked up the skill over time.

When we went to Khan Market yesterday, we expected it to be a normal day, a mere hangout but this outcome was not expected by us. It was the start of their lives and a change of ours.

Different people from two different worlds went to sleep in peace that night thinking of what could've happened if even the tiniest detail had changed. Sir Isaac Newton's first law of motion states that a body at rest will remain at rest unless acted upon by an external, unbalanced force. I felt that force on the day i went to khan market and saw those children, maybe not in the literal sense but i felt it and that was the start of a change for us as well as them.

We often think of studying as a burden, not thinking of what it means to others who have never even gotten a chance to experience it. Education is a beacon of light that illuminates paths previously disguised in the darkness of shadows.

CHAPTER 2

Getting off the flight, not at your destination, but back home. A feeling, unmatchable. Coming back home, which to me, is Delhi, makes me feel warm and welcome like a hot tea cup.

I visited one of the most beautiful parts of India, the Andaman Islands. It was extremely peaceful, as expected. The trees, the oceanic waves lapping over the sounds of the hot summer breeze, scuba diving, the little grains of sand hiding homes of unseen animals and the beautiful, flower-like patterns of the bubble crabs. Everything that resides in Andaman contributes to its beauty.

All of this aside, what captivated my mind was how clean the islands were. I thought about it for hours. The next few days there, I observed the people deeply. This cleanliness was not just because of government policies, restrictions, or rules. It was because of the genuine love the people have for these islands. They consider these Islands their home, therefore polluting them, they feel, will ruin the purity of their livelihood.

The roads, pavements, streets, markets, and even the public beaches had not a spot of bother. Tourists and

others who were littering public areas were stopped at an instant by the locals. Outsiders were cajoled and reminded again and again to clean up after their messes.

Touching and convincing boards had been placed all over the beaches. I was an absolute fan. The simple message they delivered was "Leave nothing but your footprints." That sentence struck me like lightning, and I fondly remember the moment I read it.

All of this got me thinking about my home, Delhi. A place known to be extremely polluted, littered. But why is it known to be littered, dirty, and suffocating? The answer is not overpopulation. These people could instead be an asset to the city if they did just one thing, loved it like their home.

We go to other countries for vacation. The prime purpose of a vacation? An escape. But why do we have to look for an escape miles away? Just like other parts of the world, Delhi can be a vacation paradise. A place known for its affection, warmth, and cleanliness instead of other opposing titles. We need to change our devious behavior towards the land we call home.

But why don't Delhites make this small effort? Why are we bound in the shackles of only hope? Why can't we find spots in Delhi to escape reality? This is all because of us. It is we who haven't loved this city for what it is, and let me tell you it is not nothing. It is a beautiful blend of diversity, animals, communities, different languages, the food, the markets and what not!

The simplest of Delhi to even the chaotic markets, every corner is abound with a picturesque vista. Even the

roads, the roads bound with beautiful pole lights further covered in tricolor lighting.

Hidden grace and beauty lie in Delhi, it is our job to bloom this grace and bring it to life and we shall take upon this job with pride. Let us learn to love this place, just like we love our home. Delhi is home to more people than some countries' whole population. It is an emotion. Let us keep the love alive between people and the city.

Let us embrace this place

And let us lean into the reality of our dream.

Leave nothing but
your footprints

CHAPTER 3

I slicked back the last of my hair and tied the hair tie around it exactly 3 times, like I always do. I rushed downstairs in the living room to have my daily 15-minute chit-chat with mom before school. She handed me a glass of milk which was frowned upon quite a bit but I managed to gulp it down. My eye suddenly glimpsed over her face and I was instantly hyperaware of the fact that she seemed more pumped up than usual.

She plopped down on the sofa chair and began - "I finallyyyyy found the digital marketer I was looking for for my company. Today will be her first day!" I had known her struggle with finding a person well enough to actually let out a squeak as soon as I heard her sentence.

"Great! Finally I won't have to listen to the disappointed signs of going through resumes everyday."

She gave me a little look and started laughing. Then, she started listing out all the impressive things on this digital marketer's resume. Her education, her previous jobs, who she's worked with, her impressive work and

what not. This went on for a solid 10 minutes until she was interrupted by the horn of my van which went off at exactly 7:30am everyday. Ah, my trusty van wale bhaiya, not a minute late on any day. I picked up my bag and my mom came downstairs with me to drop me off.

My van wale bhaiya rolled down his mirror and greeted my mom with his usual "Namaste ma'am." And then continued. "Ma'am I will not be in town this week. I am going somewhere with my family after dropping them off."

My mom cut him off. "That's okay Yogesh Ji, I can have my driver pick and drop her this week."

"That's not necessary ma'am I have arranged another driver for this week who will pick up and drop the kids today as well as the entire week."

"Oh. Thank you so much Yogesh Ji."

"No ma'am, not at all, this is my job. Just wanted to let you know." He rolled up his mirror and we drove off to school. We took a slight detour through a village due to road blockage at the Akshardham Temple road.

"You know beta, this was the school I studied at till grade 8th." He pointed to a small school in the village.

"Why only till grade 8 bhaiya? Why not after that?" A friend of mine pointed it out.

"Beta, my parents could not afford higher education for me." There was a slight silence that followed.

"Oh by the way, the man that will pick you up today is my younger brother. His name is Ganpath."

We reached school and spent the day like any other. At the pickup point, we found Ganpath bhaiya and sat in the car. I didn't want to sleep on the way back to help the new driver bhaiya with any guidance he might need on the way to my house but I was too tired to help it. What shocked me was that I woke up right in front of my house. I got out of the car, waved my friends bye and walked off into my house. As I filled up my plate for lunch, a

certain thought wandered my mind. Had Yogesh Ji really explained the entire route from school to each one of the 6 kids' houses just so we wouldn't have to face the most minor inconvenience for a mere 3-4 days?

I was sitting in my mom's studio, at crossroads, contemplating upon the biggest decision of the year: What to wear for Diwali. As I bobbed my head between the two beautiful draped 'anarkalis', my mom stared at me with a gaze that warned me to make my decision thereupon. She was getting impatient, not only at how indecisive and slow I was but also at the fact that her new 'professional'

digital marketer was already forty-two minutes late on her first day.

After what seemed like an eternity, I finally made my decision and my mom let out a heavy sigh. She got up and gave some instructions to her staff regarding alterations. The conversation was interrupted by the flinging open of the main door behind us. In came a young woman, probably in her mid-twenties, wearing a lousy button down hanging on top of her trousers and a frightful attempt at a hair bun. She had a plate of freshly made samosas in her hand with a purse dangling over her shoulder and she was panting as if she just ran a 20k marathon to get here. The look on my mother's face was one that never brought any good.

"You are Ayaana? The digital marketer who has a degree from NYU?" my mother asked with a firm yet disgusted voice.

"Yes ma'am, I'm so sorry for being late." She managed to get out between her heavy breathing.

My mom did nothing but stare at her ghastly, appalling behavior as she plopped down on one of the sofa chairs and asked for water as she gobbled down her samosas.

My mom was not having it as she gave me a look of horror which I returned because I was simply just as shocked as her. But I didn't want to witness the

circumstances of the situation so I slipped out of her studio into her office through the back door.

I walked into the quiet office, closing the door behind me and thought about my day since the morning. Everything that went down during this day, whether the smile on my mom's face after Yogesh bhaiya's small gesture or the look of disgust on her face upon the arrival of this professional made me question: Is it the degrees we hold or the values we embody that truly define our worth? The simplest acts of responsibility can overshadow the grandest credentials. Are these work ethics to be taught to a person? Who is someone if not their morals?

My mom came into the office with a blank expression. "Well, that was a disaster."

I shrugged indicating agreement. "I guess I'll have to go back to listening to disappointed sighs again."

She gave me a sarcastic nudge on my head and we laughed it off.

"So actually, the question is," she said, "When work ethics clash with professional achievements, which one truly prevails?"

CHAPTER 4

The hot air of Delhi blew over my face and a bead of sweat made its way down my forehead. To be honest, I wasn't sure why I was in Lodhi Garden at an hour of maximum humidity, when the sun was still harsh and the air felt heavy. Just as I was walking down the pedestrian path, taking in my surroundings- the towering trees, the historical tombs, the joggers and families out for their evening strolls- two women brushed past me, stumbling upon my feet. As I regained my balance, I couldn't help overhearing fragments of their conversation. Intrigued by their words, I slowed down my pace.

"Delhi has always been quite calm and peaceful to me." one of them said. Her voice was soft yet certain, betraying years of wisdom. She looked like she was in her sixties, her silver hair pulled back into a neat bun. There was a grace about her that suggested a lifetime spent in this city. Each step she took was a calm one, making no sound as if her sandals were padded.

"Calm and peaceful?" the younger woman scoffed, her voice incredulous. She seemed to be in her thirties with an air of briskness of someone used to navigating crowded metro platforms and traffic jams. "Delhi is a damn whirlwind, constantly in motion. It's chaotic, noisy, and it never rests. I've only been here for six years, but I can tell you, this city is exhausting!"

The older woman chuckled lightly under her breath "Ah, but that's the beauty of Delhi, my dear. You see chaos, but I see tranquility. I was born here. Sixty years of watching the seasons change, the people change, and yet, the city has remained my constant companion. I can't depend on the same people I did 20 years ago but what I can do is seek solace in the same spots I did 2 decades back. " she said with a soft smile on her face.

Their conversation struck a chord within me as I followed them at a distance, pretending to be lost in my own thoughts while eavesdropping on theirs. The younger woman shook her head in disbelief, her ponytail bouncing with each hurried step.

"When I first came here," she continued, "I felt like the city was swallowing me whole. The honking cars, the never-ending noise, the bustling crowds at Connaught Place, the pressure of work, and the heat—it was too much.

I would lie awake at night listening to the sounds of the city, wondering how anyone could call this place home. It still is extremely exhausting but now, I can't imagine living anywhere else."

The older woman nodded, a knowing smile playing on her lips. "Delhi has a way of doing that to people. It gives you what you seek, but only if you let it. If you focus on the chaos, you'll be swept away in it. But if you look for peace, you'll find that too."

I pondered their words as they drifted ahead of me, their voices growing fainter. They seemed to encapsulate the paradox that Delhi is—a city where peace and chaos coexist, each waiting to be discovered depending on what you're searching for.

As I wandered deeper into Lodhi Garden, I noticed how the greenery seemed to muffle the distant honks of the city. The ancient tombs stood tall and silent, guardians of a long-forgotten era, their stillness contrasting sharply with the bustling world outside. For a moment, it felt as though I had stepped into another time, where life moved slower, where people paused to breathe, and where the rush of modern Delhi seemed miles away. This was the peace the older woman spoke of—the quiet corners where the city holds its breath.

But I also knew the other side of Delhi. The side that pulsed with energy, where markets buzzed with life, and

where the streets were alive with the sounds of a thousand conversations happening at once. The chaos the younger woman described wasn't wrong either—it was part of the city's heartbeat. I thought of Chandni Chowk, its narrow lanes packed with vendors and shoppers, where every inch seemed alive with activity, where survival seemed to depend on your ability to navigate the madness.

The beauty of Delhi, I realized, was that it could be both things at once. For some, it was a solace of stillness, a city that offered calm wherever you looked for it. For others, it was a never-ending challenge, a place that pushed you to your limits, forced you to adapt, and offered growth through its chaos. Delhi was everything, and it had a place for everyone.

I turned to look back at the two women. They had stopped under a tree, still talking, their conversation no longer audible to me, but I imagined it continued to explore their different experiences of the same city. They were living proof of what Delhi could be—a different home for each person, shaped by their perspective, their journey and their way of comprehending it.

As I left Lodhi Garden, the heat still clinging to the air, I smiled to myself. The two women opened my eyes

and I concluded with a beautiful thought. Delhi didn't ask you to choose between peace and chaos—it gave you both. It was a city that could be as calming as the quiet of dawn at India Gate, or as overwhelming as rush hour at Rajiv Chowk. It was up to you to decide which one you wanted to embrace.

And maybe that's why, no matter where you come from or how you see it, Delhi can always be home.

EPILOGUE

Delhi is my kingdom
And my house a palace
To shield me away
From all kinds of malice

The late night drives to India Gate
Learning in school- Delhi,
India's capital state.
Not a care in the world, I'm carefree,
Don't care about anything not centered around me.
"Mom, who are those people on the street"
"Oh, that's none of your concern, honey."

But now I'm watching Delhi change
As I'm growing up.
It's a feeling certainly strange
Which brings thoughts I can't arrange.

I don't want to know more than I already understand,
I don't want to grow older than I already am.
Time has passed by without so much as a whisper in my ear,
I still haven't adjusted to it speeding by year after year.
And every year, Delhi, to me, becomes clear.

I always wonder
How a population this large
Can adjust to newness this fast
With no stopwatch.

Nearly 34 million people
Some clear about yet some unaware
Of Delhi's upheaval.
Some don't know here or there,
Some happy, some in despair.
Some lives luxurious yet some unfair.
Some living on the streets,
Just getting by bare.
And amongst all this,
No fresh air?!

This wouldn't have made sense when i was younger
When delhi was my kingdom and my house a palace
To shield me away from all kinds of malice.

I used to hear back then,
"Delhi isn't clean, there's no fresh air."
But me, a mere child, who was I to care

But now I see
I see people dying and people hungered.
I used to see only rainbows with rain,
But now I see the thunder.

And now I know that even though,
Delhi is still my kingdom
And my house, still my palace.
Not everyone is shielded away
From all kinds of malice.

ACKNOWLEDGMENTS

I want to thank my family for their unwavering support and words of affirmation which have been my foundation for motivation. Your belief in me, even when I doubted myself, has been invaluable. To my mentors, thank you for your endless advice and the occasional "you got this!" moments. And of course, to my friends, you're the reason I didn't lose my mind halfway through this. Thank you for the unending laughter and pick-me-ups when I wanted to give up myself.

LEAVE
NOTHING
BUT
YOUR
FOOTPRINTS

9 798889 744144 0